DO YOU WANT TO PLAY CATCH?

By Chris Draft

Do You Want to Play Catch?

First Edition 2010
Library of Congress Control Number: 2009942937
ISBN 978-0-9825713-2-3
Clifton Carriage House Press

Written by Chris Draft
Book Illustrations and Design by Anthony Sclavi; BRIO, Minneapolis, MN

Printed in United States of America

CLIFTON
CARRIAGE
HOUSE

THIS BOOK IS DEDICATED TO
All the parents looking for a way to connect with their kids

And all of my fellow teammates who dedicate their lives to helping others.

I play
in the
NFL.

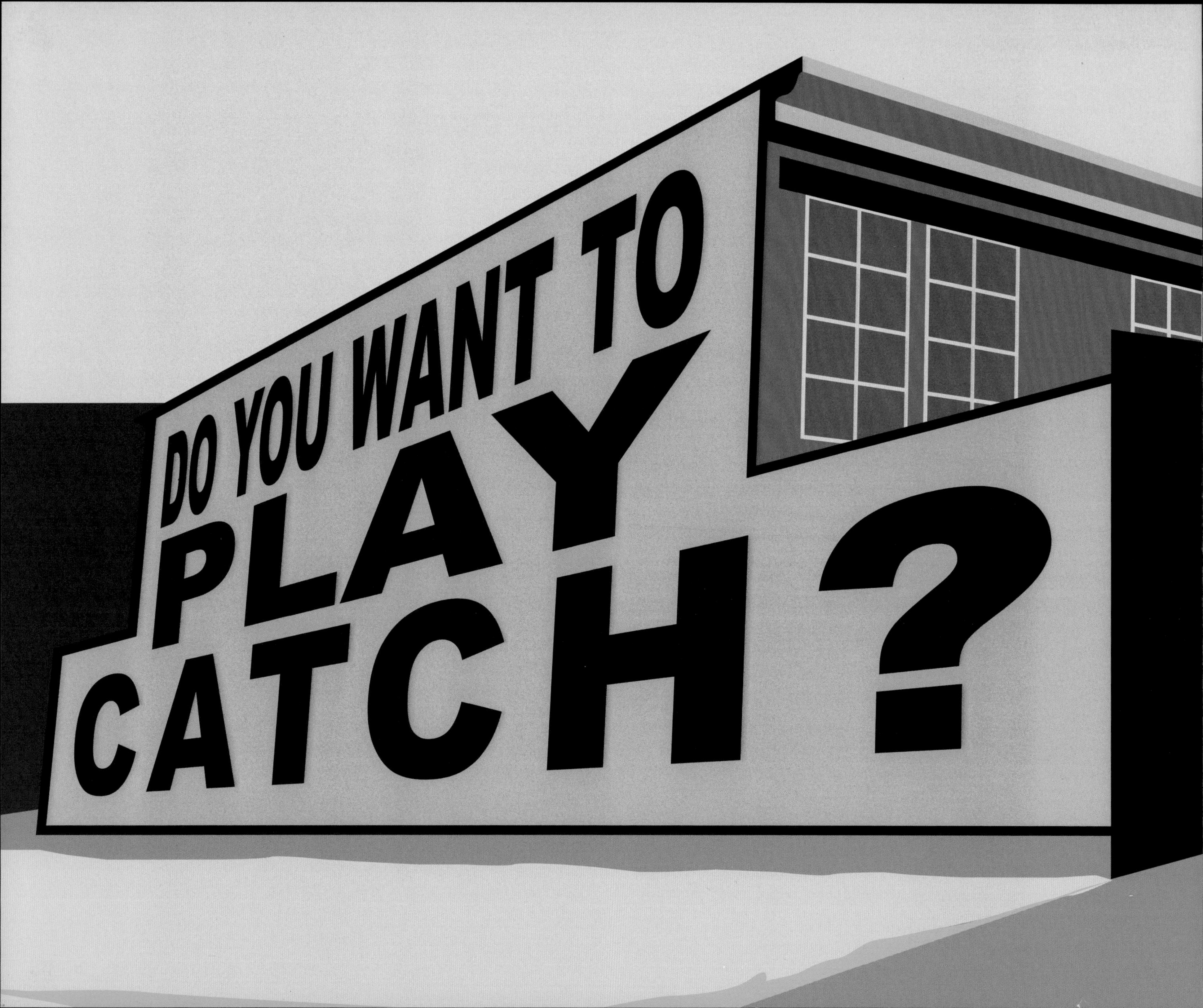
DO YOU WANT TO
PLAY
CATCH?

I hear the garage open. There's my dad.

We play catch in the alley behind the townhome.

Mom is home.

My coach said that girls can't throw because they wear bras.

Well, watch me throw this ball!

There's my brother Tony

"Hey, do you want to play catch?"

"How about some whiffle ball?"

"Let's go to the field at the school, by the first grade classrooms."

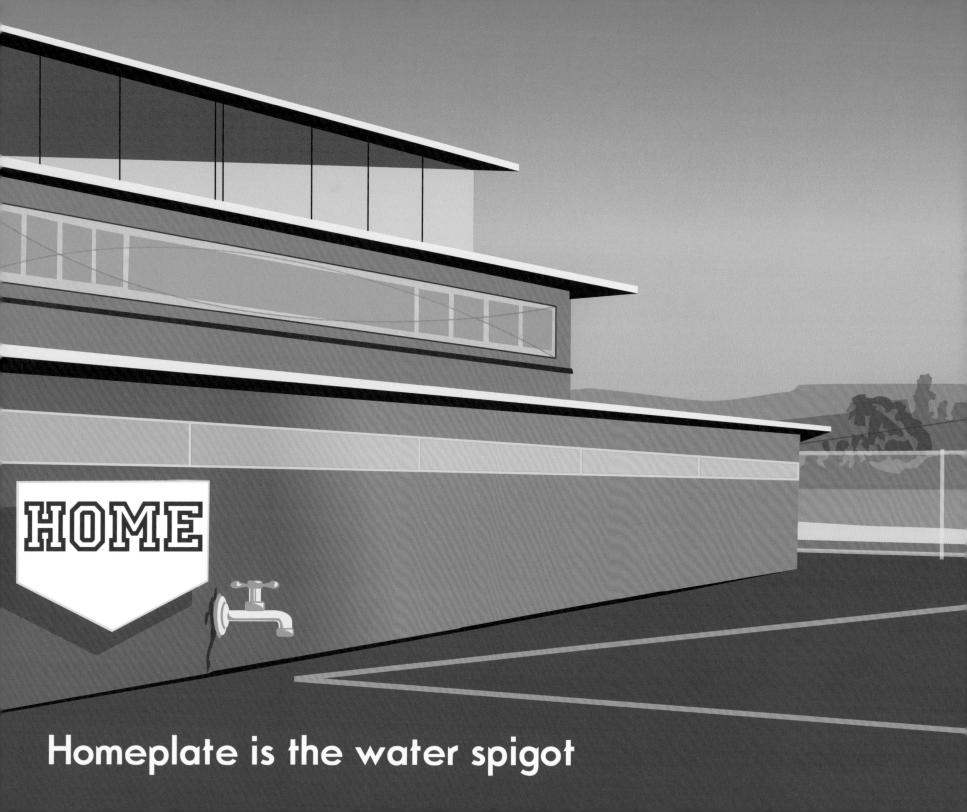

HOME

Homeplate is the water spigot

Second base is the pole in the outfield.

Third base is Oregon on the US map painted on the blacktop

2ND

3RD

1ST

First base is the first square on the hopscotch court

While playing catch, I got to know a lot about my family ...

I found out that my Dad is a salesman. A salesman of many things food related. That meant at times we had plenty of French fries, bacon, turkey and whatever other products that he was around. But the most important thing that I found out, was that my Dad will always be my coach. Not just my sports coach. My life coach.

I found out that my Mom is a social worker. A social worker that gives all her soul to her job, knowing that it is very difficult to find a bad kid. A little extra time and commitment can change a life.

I found out that one of the greatest blessings is having a brother.

Do you want to play catch?

Do you want to shoot hoop?

Do you want to play football?

Do you want to ride big wheels?

Do you want to talk until we fall asleep?

The Chris Draft Family Foundation

In 2006, NFL Veteran Linebacker and Stanford University graduate Chris Draft established the Chris Draft Family Foundation. The Foundation focuses on seven primary initiatives with overarching themes that stress the importance of education, healthy lifestyles, character development, personal responsibility, self-discipline and physical fitness.

The Foundation seeks partnerships with local and national community health organizations, school districts and non-profits across the country, striving to empower and uplift communities by educating and equipping families to make healthier choices.

Throughout most of the year, the Foundation operates out of St. Louis, home of Chris Draft and the St. Louis Rams. While the Foundation's home office is located in Atlanta, GA, the Foundation is active all across the United States, working in communities across the country from Washington D.C. to Los Angeles, California and Minnesota to Texas. The Foundation maintains a strong community presence in Chris Draft's former NFL homes: Chicago, San Francisco, Atlanta, and Charlotte, his birthplace of Kansas as well as his hometown of Anaheim, in Southern California.

Chris Draft and the Chris Draft Family Foundation travel across the United States during the NFL season, recruiting for the Foundation's Asthma Team™ and Character Team™. Throughout the year, additional events with youth and families are planned around all Foundation initiatives, including visits to military bases and hospitals, the Get Checked and Get Fit™ Draft Day® fitness camp for youth and families (traditionally held at the Super Bowl in February and in the current NFL home city in the off-season), film screenings, roundtable discussions, school visits, park clean-ups and gardening projects.

2009 marks Chris Draft's 12th year in the NFL, and his experience has shaped the Foundation's mission, goals and community work. As an active NFL player living with asthma, Chris works with national and local organizations to increase awareness of the disease with a range of PSAs and special-themed events using his personal experiences to inspire others. A health and fitness advocate, Chris designed his Draft Day® fitness camp that debuted in 2006 at the NFL YET/Atlanta aimed toward providing youth and parents with tools to make choices to live healthier lifestyles. The importance of family literacy and character education, with a focus on personal responsibility and self-discipline fuel the Foundation's major initiatives, all centered on uplifting communities and empowering families to live healthy lifestyles.

DO YOU WANT TO PLAY CATCH NOW?